CHICKEN FOR

Story by
Nettie Lowenstein
Pictures by Jonathan Hills

Published by Dinosaur Publications

Text copyright © Nettie Lowenstein 1987
Illustrations copyright © Jonathan Hills 1987

Published by Dinosaur Publications
8 Grafton Street, London W1X 3LA

Dinosaur Publications is an imprint of
Fontana Paperbacks, part of
the Collins Publishing Group

Printed by Warners of Bourne and London

The cats slept on the wall.

The cats stood on the wall.

The cats walked on the wall.

Mum and Dad sat in the kitchen.

They were talking.

They were drinking.

They were eating.

They were laughing.

The cats walked on the wall.

The cats stood on the wall.

The cats slept on the wall.

But where is the chicken?